The Owl Swings a Dowel

Anders Hanson

Consulting Editor, Diane Craig, M.A./Reading Specialist

Publishing Company

Published by ABDO Publishing Company, 4940 Viking Drive, Edina, Minnesota 55435.

Printed in the United States.

Credits
Edited by: Pam Price
Curriculum Coordinator: Nancy Tuminelly
Cover and Interior Design and Production: Mighty Media
Photo and Illustration Credits: BananaStock Ltd., Brand X Pictures, Corel, Digital Vision, Eyewire Images, Anders Hanson, Hemera, Image 100, PhotoDisc

Library of Congress Cataloging-in-Publication Data

Hanson, Anders, 1980-
    The owl swings a dowel / Anders Hanson.
       p. cm. -- (Rhyme time)
    Includes index.
    ISBN 1-59197-809-2 (hardcover)
    ISBN 1-59197-915-3 (paperback)
    1. English language--Rhyme--Juvenile literature. I. Title. II. Rhyme time (ABDO Publishing Company)

PE1517.H3783 2004
428.1'3--dc22
                                                                    2004050792

SandCastle™ books are created by a professional team of educators, reading specialists, and content developers around five essential components that include phonemic awareness, phonics, vocabulary, text comprehension, and fluency. All books are written, reviewed, and leveled for guided reading, early intervention reading, and Accelerated Reader® programs and designed for use in shared, guided, and independent reading and writing activities to support a balanced approach to literacy instruction.

Let Us Know

After reading the book, SandCastle would like you to tell us your stories about reading. What is your favorite page? Was there something hard that you needed help with? Share the ups and downs of learning to read. We want to hear from you! To get posted on the ABDO Publishing Company Web site, send us e-mail at:

sandcastle@abdopub.com

SandCastle Level: Transitional

Words that rhyme do
not have to be spelled the
same. These words rhyme
with each other:

dowel

prowl

foul

scowl

growl

towel

howl

trowel

owl

vowel

Patsy's dog is friendly.

He does not **growl** at people.

Jim had fun playing soccer in the mud.

But his face and clothes are **foul**.

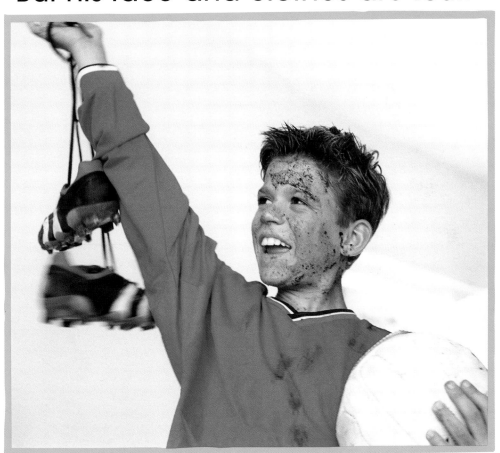

Sometimes grey wolves howl in the forest.

These clothes hangers are suspended from a **dowel**.

An **owl** can live to be 35 years old.

After swimming, Cynthia's mom wraps her in a **towel**.

These cheetahs are hungry.

They are on the **prowl**.

Lindsay likes to plant flowers.

To make planting easier, she uses a **trowel**.

Brady is upset.

He expresses his anger with a **scowl**.

The first letter of the alphabet is a **vowel**.

The Owl
Swings a Dowel

Ollie the owl
and Freddie the fowl
like to play baseball
with a wooden dowel.

For home plate, they use a towel.
They mark each base with a trowel.

It's Ollie's turn to bat.

He swings the dowel
and misses the first pitch
from Freddie the fowl.

"Strike one!" says Freddie with a growl.

17

Ollie hits the next pitch foul.

"Strike two!" shouts Freddie with a howl.

Ollie whacks the third pitch
hard with the dowel.

"Home run! Home run!"
shouts Ollie the owl.

Freddie says,
"Good for you,
Ollie the owl!

Now it's my turn
to swing that dowel!"

Rhyming Riddle

What do you call
a dirty hand shovel?

Foul trowel

Glossary

foul. extremely dirty or smelly; being outside the baselines in baseball

fowl. a bird, such as a duck, goose, turkey, or chicken, that is eaten or hunted

prowl. to move quietly or secretively in search of something

scowl. an angry look made by contracting the eyebrows

trowel. a small gardening tool with a curved blade used for digging and planting

About SandCastle™

A professional team of educators, reading specialists, and content developers created the SandCastle™ series to support young readers as they develop reading skills and strategies and increase their general knowledge. The SandCastle™ series has four levels that correspond to early literacy development in young children. The levels are provided to help teachers and parents select the appropriate books for young readers.

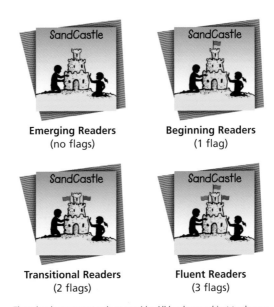

Emerging Readers
(no flags)

Beginning Readers
(1 flag)

Transitional Readers
(2 flags)

Fluent Readers
(3 flags)

These levels are meant only as a guide. All levels are subject to change.

To see a complete list of SandCastle™ books and other nonfiction titles from ABDO Publishing Company, visit **www.abdopub.com** or contact us at:
4940 Viking Drive, Edina, Minnesota 55435 • 1-800-800-1312 • fax: 1-952-831-1632